Here comes

FRANKIE!

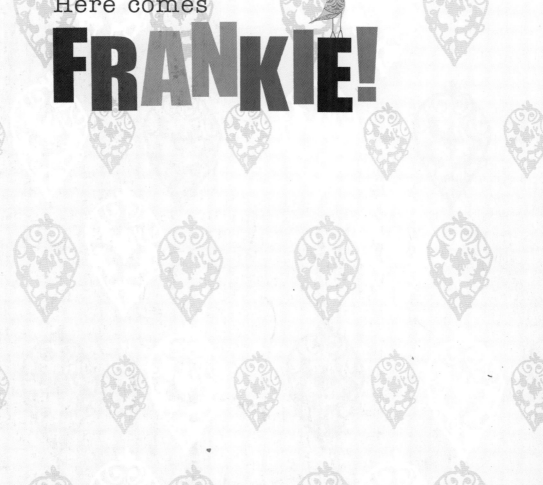

Quiet Mist

Hush Pink

Sssh! White

Fog

Gentle Grey

Tranquil White

Whisper

Murmur

Mutter Yellow

Silent Night

Peaceful Pink

Still Blue

Lullaby Green

Float

Soft Symphony

Mumble Beige

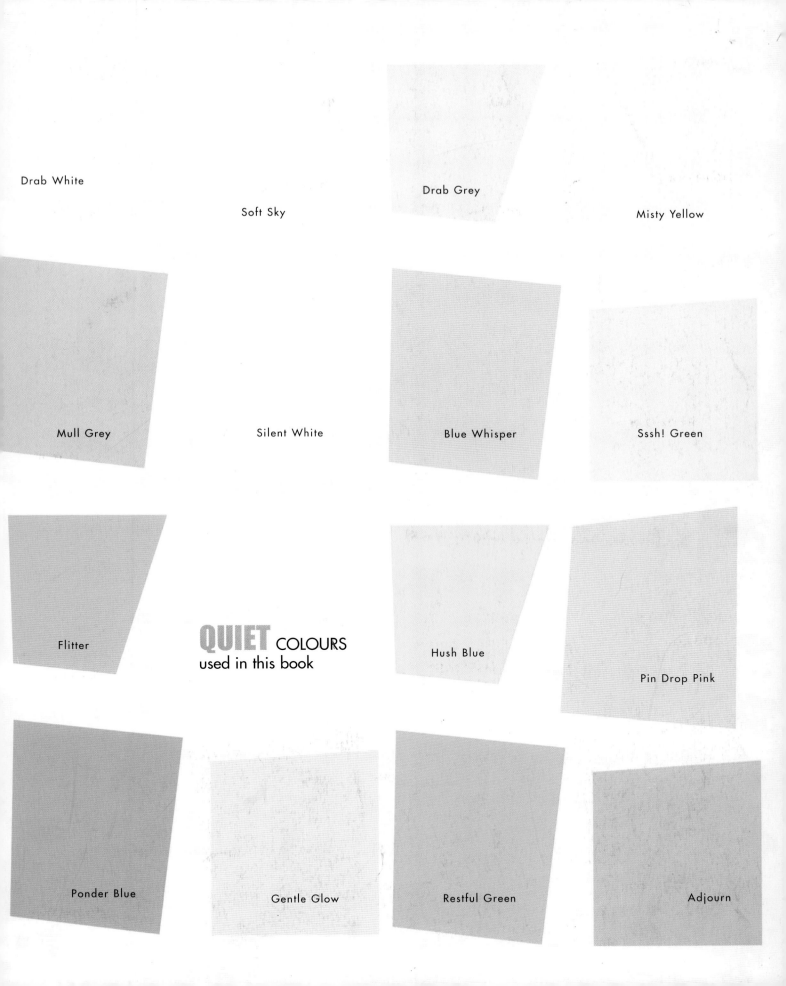

Drab White

Soft Sky

Drab Grey

Misty Yellow

Mull Grey

Silent White

Blue Whisper

Sssh! Green

Flitter

QUIET COLOURS
used in this book

Hush Blue

Pin Drop Pink

Ponder Blue

Gentle Glow

Restful Green

Adjourn

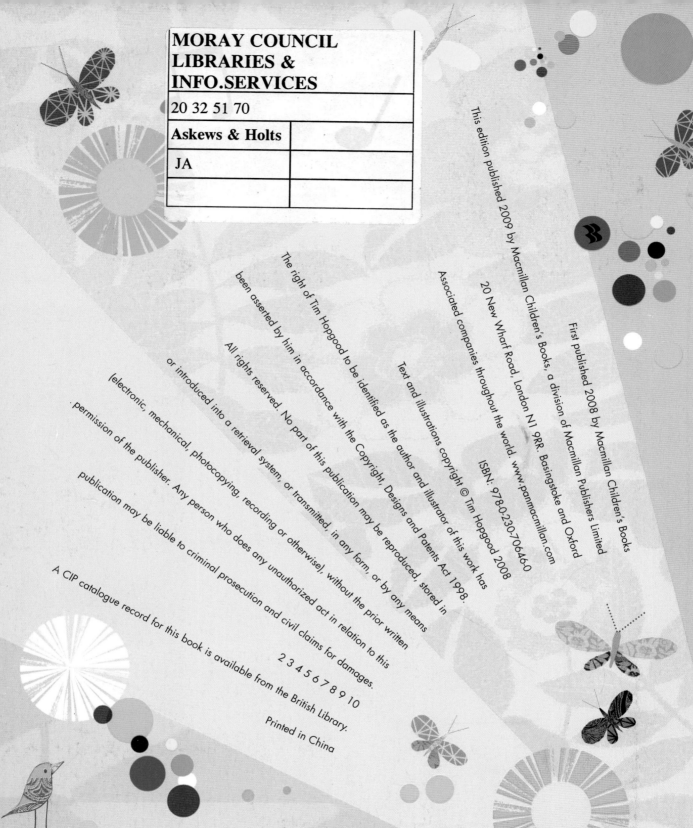

This edition published 2009 by Macmillan Children's Books, a division of Macmillan Publishers Limited

20 New Wharf Road, London N1 9RR. Basingstoke and Oxford

Associated companies throughout the world. www.panmacmillan.com

First published 2008 by Macmillan Children's Books

ISBN: 978-0-230-70646-0

Text and illustrations copyright © Tim Hopgood 2008

For Bill, in-a-bit-mate!
The Blue Sails, The Phonebook and all budding musicians young and old.

With thanks to Celia Catchpole, Emily Ford and Kayt Manson.

Here comes
FRANKIE!

timhopgood

MACMILLAN CHILDREN'S BOOKS

Frankie lived with his parents halfway along Ellington Avenue.

It wasn't the kind of street where children
played happily outside, or where the
neighbours stood and chatted.
Ellington Avenue was always very quiet.

Even the birds had lost their chirp.

Frankie had always been
quiet and well behaved.

As a baby he never cried.
As a toddler he never caused a fuss,
and at school Frankie only spoke
when he was spoken to.

Frankie's parents both worked
at the local library.

They had two family pets:
a cat called Ella that NEVER
miaowed, and a dog called
Duke that NEVER barked.

They all lived together
in perfect peace and quiet.

And that's
exactly
how Frankie's
parents liked it.

His father would read
for hours in silence,

while his mother liked doing the crossword puzzle.

But Frankie was beginning to find life at home just a little TOO quiet.

Even the big clock had lost its tick-tock.

And so, that very night, the usually quiet Frankie made a very LOUD announcement.

"I've decided," said Frankie.

"I want to learn to play the **trumpet!**"

Frankie's parents
looked rather worried.

**"I've a lovely book
on trumpets you can
look at,"** said his mother,
hopefully.

**"I don't want to read
about trumpets,"**
said Frankie.
**"I want to PLAY
the trumpet."**

"Now listen, son,"
said his father.
**"How about learning
to play something
quiet, like chess?"**

But chess was too
quiet for Frankie.

And Frankie was too
fidgety for chess.

A few days later,
Frankie marched home
from school with a
shiny trumpet
under his arm.

As soon as he was indoors, he put the trumpet to his mouth, puffed up his cheeks and **blew,**

and **blew,**
and **blew,**

until he was **blue** in the face.

But not a single **toot** or even a small **peep** came out of Frankie's trumpet.

So Frankie tried again . . .

Suddenly there came a small squeak,

then a LOUD parp

and a nasty ear-splitting sound.

Frankie rubbed his eyes and wrinkled his nose.

The whole room was the colour of **dirty dishwater** and smelt like **pickled onions!**

"Frankie!
Frankie!
I can't hear myself
think," called his father.
"And whatever is
that awful stink?"

"I think it's next
door's drains,"
his mother replied.

But it wasn't.
It was coming from
Frankie's trumpet!

Frankie was amazed.

When he played the trumpet he could not only **hear** the sounds, but he could **see** and **smell** them too!

coffee

burnt toast

sausages

cherry

The **lower** the note,
        the **darker** the colour.

apple

orange

pineapple

lemon

The **higher** the note,
the **lighter** the colour.

The more Frankie played, the more
colours and smells appeared.

banana

pear

mint

So he practised and practised until . . .

The air was filled with **colourful** music and bursts of **weird** and **wonderful** smells.

strawberry

mint

cherry

sweaty feet

stinky cheese

hot dog

coconut

apple & pear

pineapple & orange

lemon

banana

kiwi fruit

Beautiful patterns of sound
floated through the house.

"Amazing!"
said his father,
putting down
his book.

"Delicious!"
cried his mother,
putting down her pen.
"And what a lovely tune.
Frankie, is that you?"

Frankie's parents couldn't believe their ears, their noses or their eyes!

Duke started to **bark,**

Ella started to **miaow,**

and the clock began to **tick-tock!**

Then Frankie's parents started to **dance.**

Frankie opened the front door and blew his trumpet as hard as he could.

As he played, the air became sweeter
and **everything** started to change.

And the **louder** Frankie played,
the **brighter** everything became.

As he marched down the street,
people came out of their houses . . .

They started to **tap** their feet, **clap** their hands
and **dance** to the sound of sunshine,

along **noisy** Ellington Avenue.

Did **YOU** know?
For some people music really does have a colour,
shape and smell. This mixing of the senses is called
Synaesthesia.
The composer **Jean Sibelius**
is said to have seen notes and smelled them too!
Other well-known synaesthetes include:
The jazz trumpeter **Miles Davis**
and the abstract painter
Wassily Kandinsky.

Cool Crunch

Amber Groove

Swing Blue

Solo Blue

Dizzy Yellow

Parker Pink

LOUD COLOURS
used in this book

Verve

Gillespie Green

Quincy Tangerine

Boogie-Woogie

So What Yellow

Chet Crimson

Holiday

Flip

Jump

Bruback Purple

Hancock Green

Bebop

A Kind Of Blue

Crush

Hi-Fi

Coltrane Blue

Shout

Nina

Birdland Yellow

Summertime Yellow

Courtney Lime